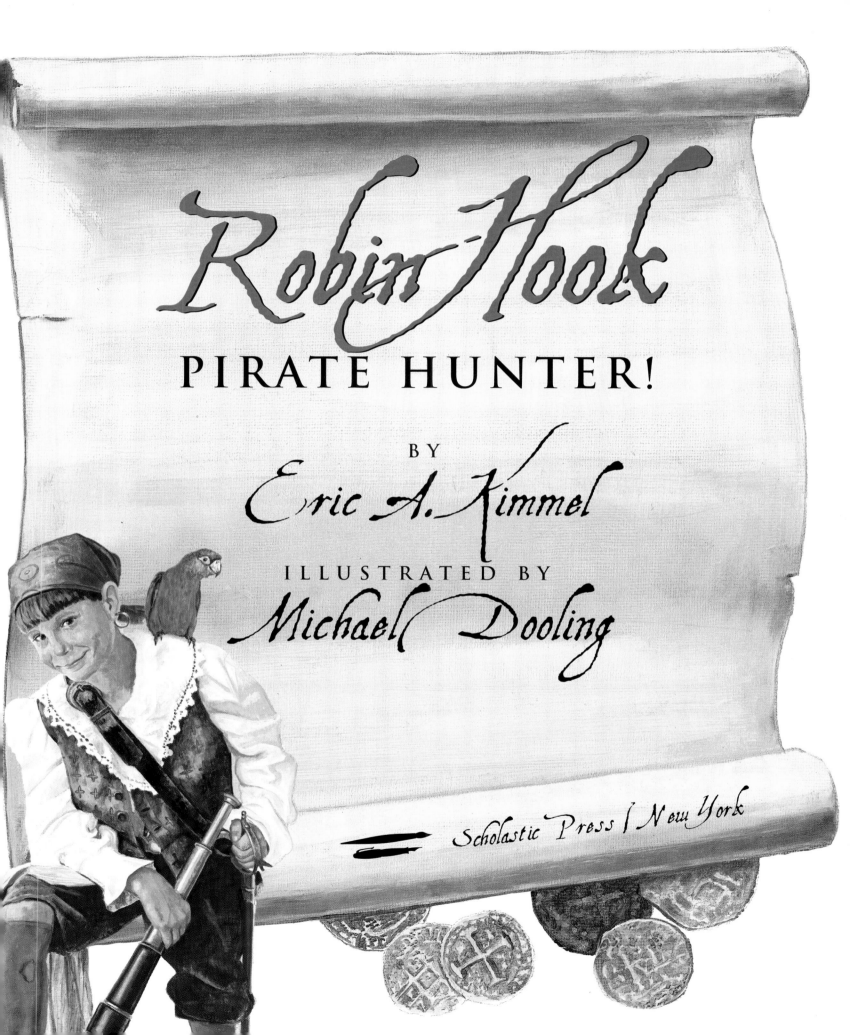

Robin Hook
PIRATE HUNTER!

BY

Eric A. Kimmel

ILLUSTRATED BY

Michael Dooling

Scholastic Press / New York

LIBRARY OF CONGRESS CATALOGING-IN-PUBLICATION DATA

Kimmel, Eric A.
Robin Hook, pirate hunter! / by Eric A. Kimmel; illustrated by Michael Dooling—1st ed.   p. cm.
Summary: A kind and honest young pirate and his ragamuffin crew thwart evil pirates by rescuing
and giving riches to the innocent and the poor.

ISBN 0-590-68199-0

[1. Pirates—Fiction.] I. Dooling Michael, ill. II. Robin Hood (Legend) III. Title.
PZ7.K5648 Ro 2001   [E]—dc21   00-035771

10 9 8 7 6 5 4 3 2 1   01 02 03 04 05

Printed in Singapore   46

First edition, March 2001

The display type was set in Aqualine.
The text type was set in 14-point Goudy.
The paintings were done in oil on canvas.
Book design by Marijka Kostiw

WINDWARD PASSAGE

TORTUGA

COVE

PORT ROYAL

THE SCALE OF MILES

To Toni Scott
E. A. K.

To my mom
M. D.

Atlantic Ocean

Hispaniola

foulground

swamp

ROBIN'S ISLAND

BAY

strong tide here

Caribbean Sea

Robin Hook, the pirate hunter! Every

seafarer knows his name. Our story begins at sea, when Captain
James Hook, a notorious pirate, finds baby Robin being rocked
in the arms of a giant octopus. There's something unusual about
this child, *thought Captain Hook. After a bitter fight with the*
octopus, he hoisted Robin aboard and raised him to be a pirate.

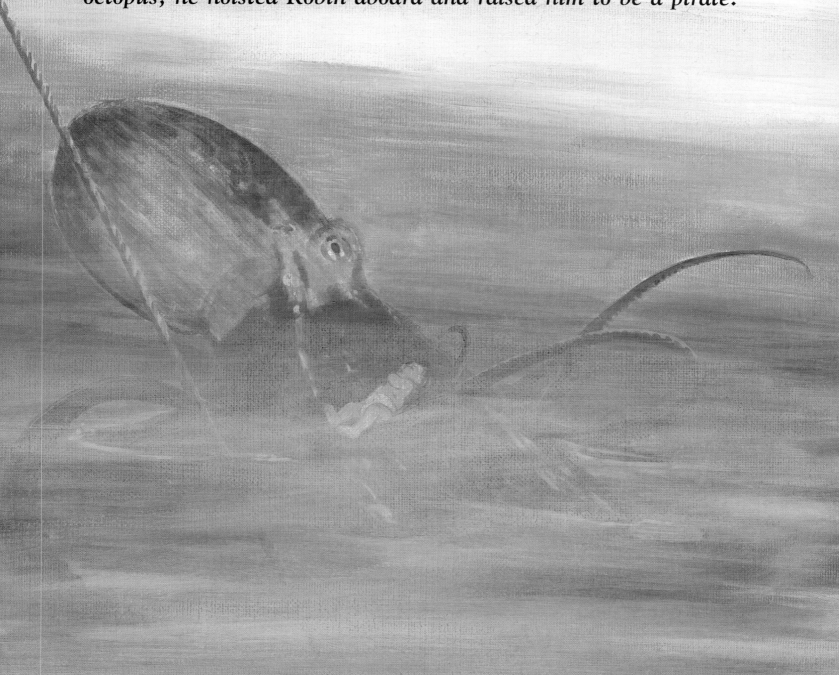

But as Robin grew up, it became apparent that he wasn't like the other pirates. He hated making people walk the plank. He never enjoyed sinking ships. And he was kind to people and animals.

Then came the time Robin helped three prisoners escape in the ship's jolly boat.

"I did it," Robin confessed to Captain Hook, "and I'll do it again!"

"This is the last straw!" bellowed Captain Hook. "These prisoners would have brought a princely ransom!"

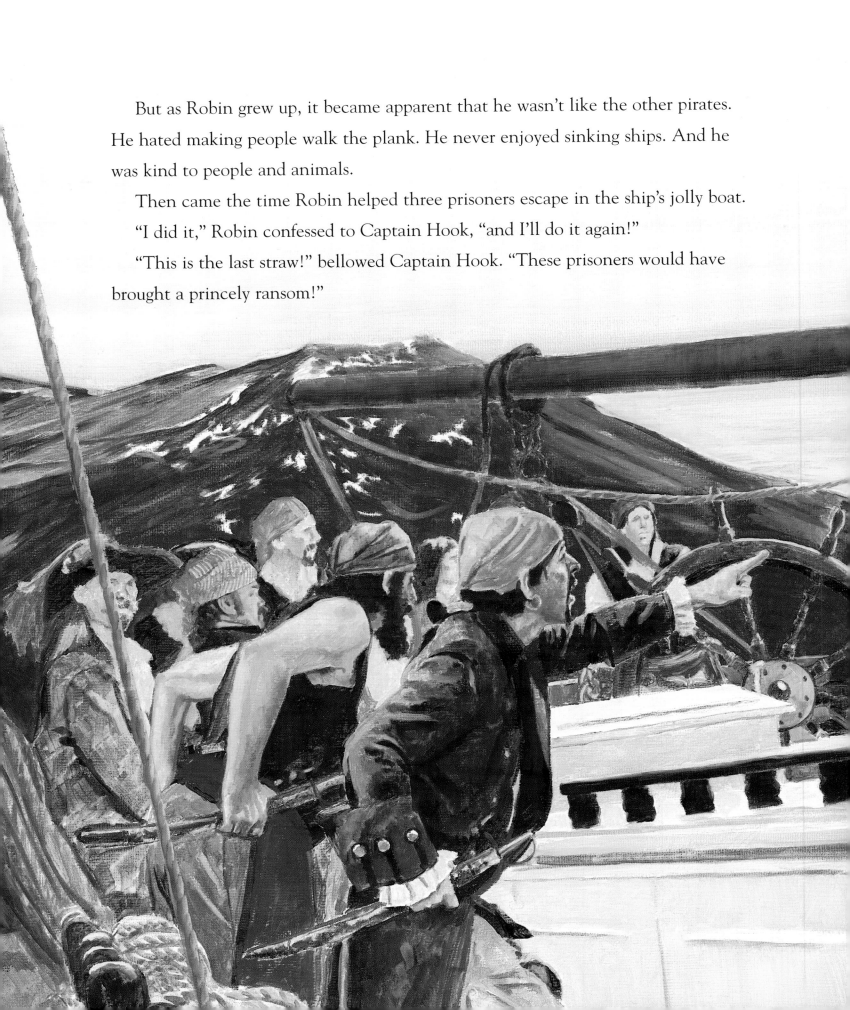

That very night, the pirates marooned Robin on a deserted island.

Those pirates! They were nothing but ruffians and bullies. As the lonely days passed into weeks, then months, Robin swore he would find a way to drive them all from the sea. He filled the hours by learning the languages of animals, and the island's creatures promised to help him.

One morning, Robin discovered children walking along the beach. They told him how a wicked pirate crew had captured their ship and marooned them on the island, too.

"Don't be afraid," Robin told them. "I'm glad you're here. We'll fight the pirates together."

Robin taught the children how to gather fruits, how to speak to the animals, and to respect all living creatures. Working together, they built a sailing ship from the trees and vines that grew in the rain forest. They christened it the *Sandpiper*. The children chose Robin to be their captain, and they became fast friends. And with his crew and the island's creatures, Robin began his campaign to bring pirates everywhere to justice.

With courage and cunning, the children slipped aboard pirate ships all over the bounding main. They hid a powerful magnet on Captain Bellamy's ship so that his compass always pointed south instead of north. They put itching powder in Blackbeard's beard, and they erased the "X" on Captain Flint's treasure map so that he would never find the buried treasure.

Pirates everywhere feared Robin and his crew. When something went wrong, they cried, "Avast! Robin Hook has struck again!"

Unfortunately, Robin never saw the heavily armed ship that slipped past his island in the dark. She was the *Avenger*, commanded by Captain Thatch, the fiercest pirate on the seven seas.

The pirates sailed unseen through the moonless night. They dropped anchor at Port Royal, the richest harbor on the Spanish Main. Then the pirates rowed ashore and spread silently through the sleeping town.

When they had stolen every last piece of gold and treasure, the rowdy pirates built a huge bonfire. They burned the judge's bench, the church pulpit, and all the books in the library. Then they paraded through the streets, flaunting their stolen finery.

At dawn, the pirates ferried their captives out to the pirate ship. They would be sold as slaves.

"If only Robin Hook were here!" an old woman wailed.

"*Awwk! Robin Hook! Robin Hook!*"

"Who said that?" Captain Thatch turned pale as he peered into the rigging.

A green parrot perched on the main yard and squawked the dreaded name.

"Robin Hook! Robin Hook!"

Captain Thatch fired his pistol, but the parrot flew away.

Then the *Avenger* weighed anchor and sailed off.

Meanwhile, Robin and his crew had just returned to their island from a harrowing pirate hunt on Skeleton Island, when the green parrot flew down and perched on Robin's shoulder.

"*Awwk!* Pirates!" the parrot squawked.

Robin sat up with a start.

"Captain Thatch! *Awwk!* In Port Royal! Taking prisoners! Come quick! *Awwk!*"

Robin climbed down from the tree. "We'll sail at once," he said. "I'll gather the crew."

Robin blew into a conch shell and summoned his crew from all corners of the island. They came by foot and by boat, by parasail and vine, and riding on the back of a giant crane.

"Captain Thatch is back!" Robin shouted. "He's taken prisoners! We must catch him before he escapes! Who's for a fight?"

The crew answered as one.

"I am!" they cried.

The *Sandpiper* sailed with the tide. Friendly dolphins guided her through the treacherous reefs. Flocks of seabirds helped Polly scan the ocean for pirates.

An albatross swooped over Polly's head. It rattled its beak to get her attention, then pointed toward the horizon.

"Sail ho! Three points to port! *Awwk!*" the green parrot squawked.

Robin aimed his telescope. The Jolly Roger, the pirate flag, flapped in the wind. "It's the *Avenger*! Clap on all sail!"

The *Sandpiper* soon drew up alongside the pirates.

"Ahoy, Captain Thatch," Robin called.

"Blast my eyes!" croaked Captain Thatch. "It's Robin Hook—and his brat crew. Give 'em a broadside, lads! Blow those babies back to kindergarten!"

But Robin and his crew were too quick for Captain Thatch. Robin blew on his conch shell. Instantly, schools of flying squid hurled themselves at the pirates, squirting blinding jets of black ink. Seagulls dived at them from the air. A cloud of hornets flew from their nests in the rigging while the *Sandpiper*'s crew cheered.

Attacked by squid, seagulls, and hornets, the pirates never noticed the dolphins nudging their ship toward the reef. The *Avenger* shuddered as she ran aground on the sharp coral. The sea rushed through her broken timbers.

"Surrender!" Robin shouted. "You're sinking!"

"Never!" roared Captain Thatch. "If we drown, the prisoners go down with us!"

Robin could not let that happen. "Take the longboat and the treasure. Let the prisoners go."

The pirates were delighted. "The gold is ours," they crowed. "We'll steal another ship when we reach Tortuga."

The pirates released the prisoners from the hold. They swam for their lives away from the sinking pirate ship.

"Bless you for saving us, Robin!" they murmured as Robin and his crew helped them aboard the *Sandpiper*.

Meanwhile, the pirates loaded the *Avenger*'s longboat with treasure. Captain Thatch urged them on with a rope's end. The *Avenger* was sinking fast.

"All hands abandon ship!" he cried. The pirates scurried onto the longboat as the *Avenger* slipped beneath the waves.

Captain Thatch sat in the stern, gnawing on a greasy sausage.

"Farewell, Robin!" he bellowed. "I trust we'll meet again." He tossed the sausage's gristly end over the side. He didn't notice the school of sharks swimming below the boat. Nothing attracts sharks like greasy sausage.

A great white shark leaped from the water. The pirates vanished in a froth of foam.

The sharks and dolphins helped recover the treasure from the shallow bottom. When it was all aboard, the *Sandpiper* set a course for Port Royal. The whole town turned out to celebrate Robin's victory.

"Huzzah! Huzzah! Huzzah!" everyone cried. "Long live Robin Hook and his brave crew!"

But Robin and his friends took little time to celebrate. As long as pirates roamed the seven seas, they knew there was still work to be done.

At dawn, Robin Hook and his brave crew said good-bye and set sail for their next adventure.

And as the *Sandpiper* disappeared into the wind, only their
song could be heard:

Wherever pirates sail the sea —
Yo-ho-ho and a rum-tum-tum!
Robin Hook and his crew will be —
Yo-ho-ho and a rum-tum-tum!
We fear no blade nor cannonball.
We help the helpless, that's our call.
It's all for one and one for all —
Watch out, pirates! Here we come!